# STRANGERS ON NMA-6

## BY HARRIETTE S. ABELS

**Library of Congress Cataloging in Publication Data**

Abels, Harriette Sheffer.
  Strangers on NMA-6
  (Galaxy I)
  SUMMARY: The theft of nickel ingots from asteroid NMA-6 provides a
puzzling mystery until members of spaceship EM 88 step in to investigate.
  (1. Science fiction) I. Title. II. Series.
PZ7.A1595St                    (Fic)                    79-4627
ISBN 0-89686-027-2


**International Standard Book Numbers:**
0-89686-027-2 Library Bound
0-89686-036-1 Paperback

**Library of Congress
Catalog Card Number:**
79-4627

## CRESTWOOD HOUSE

**P.O. Box 3427**
**Hwy. 66 South**
**Mankato, MN 56001**

# STRANGERS ON NMA-6

## BY HARRIETTE S. ABELS

### ILLUSTRATED BY RODNEY AND BARBARA FURAN

### EDITED BY DR. HOWARD SCHROEDER

Professor in Reading and Language Arts
Dept. of Elementary Education
Mankato State University

### DESIGNED BY BARBARA FURAN

## About the author . . .

Harriette Sheffer Abels was born December 1, 1926 in Port Chester, New York. She attended Furman University, Greenville, South Carolina for one year. In addition to having her poetry published in the Furman literary magazine, she had her first major literary success while at the University. She wrote, produced and directed a three act musical comedy that was a smash hit!

At the age of twenty she moved to California, where she worked as a medical secretary for four years. In September, 1949, she married Robert Hamilton Abels, a manufacturers sales representative.

She began writing professionally in September, 1963. Her first major story was published in **Highlights For Children** in March, 1964, and her second appeared in **Jack and Jill** a short while later. She has been selling stories and articles ever since. Her first book was published by Ginn & Co., for the Magic Circle Program, in 1970.

Harriette and her husband love to travel and are looking forward to their annual trip to Europe. While travel doesn't leave much time for writing, Harriette does try to write at least something every day. When at home a sunporch serves as her office, but she confesses that most of her serious writing is done while stretched out on her bed.

The Abels have three children - Barbara Heidi, David Mark, and Carol Susan, and three dogs - Coco, Bon Bon, and Ginger Ale.

# STRANGERS ON NMA-6

Asteroid NMA-6 moved ahead in space. Aboard Emergency Spaceship EM 88, the crew prepared to dock. Druce, captain of the EM 88, was in his command cabin. He flipped on the intercom.

"How much longer, Brita?" he asked.

His pilot answered immediately. "We should be docking in an hour," she said.

Fifty minutes later, Brita guided the huge spacecraft into the asteroid dock.

When everything was secure, Druce turned on the general intercom system.

"Attention, everyone," he commanded. "We are docked at NMA-6. This is not a planet or an Astro-orb. This is an asteroid. Anyone leaving the ship must wear a spacesuit. Exit will be through the third level tunnel only. There will be a constant watch on the transition tunnel. Please do not leave unless you have to. Work crews report to the loading area. Work detail should begin by 1600."

He glanced down and checked his compu-watch.

"It is now 1400. Work detail, stand by for further orders."

Druce picked up his spacesuit and went up to the first level of the ship. He walked into the pilot's cabin. Brita and her co pilot, Joris, were getting ready to leave.

"Are you going out and take a look around?" Druce asked.

"If you don't mind, sir," Joris said.

"Wait for me. I'm going, too," Rina, the ship's navigator, called from her small office.

"All right," Druce agreed. "But remember, there are no domes on asteroids. You must wear a spacesuit at all times."

"This is my first stop on an asteroid," Joris said. "Is it as big as an Astro-orb?"

"Some of them are," Druce said. "But not this one. This one is only about three kilometers wide.

"And they mine here?" Joris asked.

"That's right," Druce nodded. "This asteroid is rich in nickel. It supplies most of the Earth's needs every year. Come on. I'll show you how it operates."

The four of them left the pilot's cabin and went down to the transition tunnel on the third level. They put on their spacesuits and left the EM 88.

Asteroid NMA-6 was cold and bleak. The surface was gray and pitted.

"It looks like the moon," Joris said.

Druce agreed. "The material that makes it up is very similar."

Joris pointed to a tall building. "What is that?"

"That's the mobile base," Druce explained. "The laboratory is in there." He pointed several hundred meters to the left. "And that is the main base, where the workers live while they are here."

Joris looked around him and shivered. "I wouldn't want to be here very long. There's nothing but space all around you."

"The miners aren't here very long," Druce said. "The whole operation usually lasts only a year to a year-and-a-half, and they change crews often. They have to. Come on, let's go find Orel."

Brita, Joris and Rina followed him toward the main base.

"Is Orel in charge here?" Brita asked.

Druce nodded. "I've met her before. This is her third assignment on an asteroid. She's supposed to be the best."

They entered the small one-room building that served as the headquarters of NMA-6.

9

Orel was seated behind her desk. She stood as they came into the room and came to greet them.

"Druce." She stuck out her hand. "It's good to see you again."

They touched hands although each was wearing the gloves of their spacesuits.

Druce introduced his crew members to her.

Orel sat down again. "I never thought I would need you, Druce. This is the first time I've had an emergency like this. But there's something strange going on."

"We're here to help," Druce said. "That's our job."

"I thought we were here to make a pickup," Brita said. "That's what my instructions said."

"That's right," Orel agreed. "But we don't usually deliver ore by spaceship."

"I wondered about that," Joris said. "I thought it was moved by transfer orbit."

"It is," Orel said. "We have always sent the ore back that way."

She pointed out of a window toward the mobile base. "We have solar furnaces. We do the smelting right here on the asteroid. Then we shoot the ingots back to headquarters Astro-orb, where they are programmed for Earth descent."

"What's the problem?" Brita asked.

"We don't know," Orel replied. "The system

has worked for hundreds of years. But suddenly, the ingots are falling out of orbit. At least," she added, "we think that's what's happening."

"That is impossible!" Druce exclaimed. "It's against all the physical laws."

Orel looked puzzled. "Exactly. We have traced every shipment we can. We have monitored them through their journey, and everything is fine. But the minute we stop, we start losing them again."

"That doesn't sound like gravity problems," Rina offered. "That sounds like human problems."

"We've thought of that, too," Orel said.

"We've put a watch on everything." She stood and began pacing back and forth. "We've tried everything we can think of. "Why —" she threw out her hands, "why would anyone want to steal ingots of nickel and iron? What could they do with them? We supply the Earth government, and there's plenty to go around."

Druce stood up, too. "There has to be an answer to this," he said. "We'll do what we can."

"I'll show you how we mine here," Orel offered.

They went back out to the bare surface of the asteroid.

"We take a core sample first," Orel explained. "I'll show you how it's done."

When they reached the mobile base, she cut out a sample with a special kind of wrench. She showed the piece of rock to Joris.

"When we first decide to mine an asteroid," Orel said, "we take many core samples like this. They're taken back to Earth and analyzed. Then they tell us what they want and how much."

"Dolf would be interested in this," Druce said. "Joris, go and get him. I don't know how much experience he's had with this kind of mining."

He turned to Orel. "Dolf is the geologist on our ship. I think he would be interested in what you're doing here."

Joris went back to the EM 88 and returned in a few moments with the young geologist.

"Dolf, look at this." Druce cut out another sample with the wrench. Then he told Dolf why they were there.

"We'll have the crews start loading as soon as you're ready," Druce said to Orel. "In the meantime, let's take a look around and see what we can find out."

Orel escorted them around the mobile base, explaining how the ingots were made. She showed them the shipping area where the ingots were launched into space.

"Timing is the important thing," she explained. "We load the space tug and put it in orbit. It pushes the ingots to the Astro-orb. When the tug returns, it has our supplies in it."

"Great system!" Joris said. "Very efficient!"

"Yes," Orel agreed. "And up until now, it has worked perfectly. Now, all of a sudden . . ." She shook her head, puzzled.

"There has to be a human hand in this someplace," Rina repeated.

Orel checked a cargo tug. "This one is just about filled, Druce. I think your people can begin loading."

"Good." Druce ordered Joris back to the ship to alert the work crew. "Get them over here and we'll begin."

"Do you mind if I look around?" Dolf asked. "This is the first time I've seen an asteroid since I was in training."

"Go right ahead," Orel said.

"I'll go with you," Rina said. "I've never landed on an asteroid before."

They wandered off, and as soon as the work detail appeared, Druce began supervising the loading operation.

When the ingots were aboard the EM 88, he went looking for Dolf and Rina.

"We're ready to leave," he said when he found them.

"Druce, are you coming back for another load?" Dolf asked.

"Yes, we'll be back in about a week," Druce answered. "We leave this load at headquarters and come back for another until the problem has been solved."

"If you don't mind, sir," Dolf said, "Rina and I would like to stay until you return."

Druce stared at him. "What are you planning?"

Dolf shook his head. "We don't honestly know. But we've talked to a few of the people here. No one can figure out why this is happening. The push into orbit is scientifically planned. There isn't any way they can be getting lost in space."

"But do you think you're the one to investigate?" Druce asked. "You're a geologist, not an astronomer or a space technician."

Dolf's laugh came from behind his helmet.

"Right," he said. "But nobody knows more about rocks than I do."

He stomped his boot lightly on the hard surface.

"It's possible that someone is interested in something besides the nickel or iron."

"But that's all that's missing," Druce answered. "They don't disappear until the smelting is done."

"There seems to be some question about that," Dolf said. "One of the men says that he thinks rock samples are also disappearing."

Druce looked at Rina. "And you're going to stay with Dolf? How am I going to run my ship without a navigator?"

"Oh Druce, come on," she argued. "Joris and Brita are perfectly capable of getting you back to Astro-orb headquarters. You're not venturing out into space. I decided to stay with Dolf because I thought with my supersight, I might be of help."

Druce nodded. "That's true. Most people don't know that you have supersight."

"The only way anyone would know was if I told them I was a navigator," Rina said. "And I don't plan on doing that."

"All right, you can stay," Druce decided. "We'll be back in about one week. But at that time I expect you both to rejoin the crew."

"By that time," Dolf said, "we hope to have figured out what's going on up here."

They returned to the asteroid's main base and explained their decision to Orel. She agreed that having Dolf and Rina there might be a big help.

"But we won't tell anyone who you really are," she said to Rina. "Let the crew think you are both geologists interested only in the rock."

When Druce and the EM 88 had taken off for headquarters Astro-orb, Orel showed Rina and Dolf to their quarters. They were each assigned a room.

"Remember," Orel warned them, "you must wear spacesuits at all times on the surface of the asteroid. Only the living quarters and the mobile base have life support systems."

Dolf and Rina set out to acquaint themselves with the entire asteroid. Scattered around were small groups of workers mining the stone from the surface. Dolf and Rina spoke to several of the groups. Some of the workers were from Earth. Some had been brought from the planet colonies.

"I've been a miner all my life," one man told them. His name was Zelig. "I was born on Mars. Earth has had mining operations there for years."

Dolf looked around at the other groups.

"I guess you're all experienced miners," he commented.

"All the ones I know are," Zelig agreed.

Rina laughed. "You mean you don't know everyone here? Surely on such a small place . . ."

She looked around. It was almost possible to see the limits of the asteroid.

"That's true," Zelig said. "And some of us have worked together before in other mining operations. But this time, we have some strangers."

"Who are they?" Dolf asked.

Zelig raised his shoulders. "We don't know. They keep pretty much to themselves. There they are. Over there."

He pointed to five spacesuited figures busy working a few meters away.

"And they have three others who work in the mobile lab," Zelig went on. "They stick pretty much to themselves. In fact, we don't even know what they look like."

"But that's impossible," Rina sputtered. "Don't you see them when they go into the living quarters?"

"No." Zelig shook his head. "They don't bunk with us. They came in their own ship. It's docked at the other end of the asteroid. They live on that."

"But Orel must know who they are," Dolf interrupted.

"If she does, she isn't saying," Zelig said.

He shook his head and turned back to his work.

"I don't understand why Orel didn't mention the strangers before," Rina said. "I think we should go have a talk with her."

They hurried back to the main base headquarters. When they told Orel what Zelig had said, she smiled.

"Of course I know who they are," she said. "They're a special group sent up here from Universe headquarters in Omaha."

"Why do they live on their own ship?" Dolf asked.

Orel shrugged. "That was the way they wanted it. I think they had instructions from Omaha. I don't really care. They don't have to mix with the other workers. Conversation isn't easy while they're working, because of the spacesuits. It's only during recreation time that the workers do things together."

"Do you have a written record of when the losses happened?" Rina asked.

Orel looked startled. "No. I never thought —"

"Would it be possible to make one up?" Dolf asked.

"Of course. We know exactly which shipments are missing."

She hurried over to a small computer standing on a table across the room. She pushed a lever. In a few seconds, she removed a long, thin tape.

"Here they are."

She gave the tape to Dolf.

He glanced quickly over it. "There doesn't seem to be any pattern to it," he said.

Rina was looking over his shoulder. "No," she agreed. "My idea was wrong."

"What did you think it was?" Dolf asked.

"I thought maybe they were disappearing at night," Rina said. "If everyone else was in the living quarters and it was dark, it would be easy for the strange crew to do whatever it is they're doing. If

they are the ones doing it."

"But that isn't what's happening," Orel explained. "We are launching them correctly. But they are disappearing on their way to headquarters."

Dolf and Rina looked surprised. "We didn't understand," Dolf said. "And you have tracked them as they're going through space?"

"Yes," Orel said. "But it's impossible to track every shipment. The ones that we do track arrive safely. As soon as we stop . . ."

"Just a minute," Rina said. "Orel, can you tell me which of the shipments were tracked?"

"I think so."

Orel went back to the computer and started it again. "Yes," she said in a moment. "We do have a record of the tracking."

Rina marked off the ones that had been tracked. "Maybe this will tell us something," she said to Dolf.

"Why don't you take that desk over there,"

Orel said. "I have to get on with my work."

Dolf and Rina sat down with the tapes in front of them. They studied them for a long time.

"There doesn't seem to be any pattern," Dolf said finally.

"Just a moment," Rina said softly. "I'm not so sure. Here. Look at this."

She pointed at several of the missing shipments.

"They all happened at a certain time," she said. "There isn't any pattern to the days, but there is to the hours. The lost shipments were always launched about 0600." She looked up at Dolf. "Probably the first shipment in the morning."

She called across the room to Orel. "We have a question."

"What is it?" Orel asked.

"What time do you begin working?"

"We start at 0600," Orel answered.

"How can you start at 0600 and launch your first tug at the same time?" Rina wondered.

"Because we fill one the last thing the night before," Orel explained.

"How many launches a day do you make?" Dolf asked.

"We try to make three," Orel said. "We have to launch so that we hit the transfer orbit correctly to headquarters Astro-lab."

Rina jumped up. "Then that's it," she said. "For some reason, the lost shipments have to be launched at 0600."

"You mean there is a pattern to it." Orel sounded excited.

"Well," Rina gave a little laugh, "it's not a definite pattern. And it may be just one of those things, but it is always the first shipment of the day that gets lost."

"I think it's time we found out more about that strange crew," Dolf said. "I'm going over and talk to them."

"Oh, Dolf, do you really think . . ." Orel began.

"We have to start somewhere, Orel," he said. "And a strange crew, who doesn't mix with the others, well —" He made a small motion with his hand. "It does seem odd."

"I agree," Rina said. "That's the logical place to begin. I'm going with you."

They went back out onto the asteroid surface and found the group they were looking for. They asked the workers a few questions.

"Who are you?" one of the workers wanted to know.

"I'm a geologist," Dolf explained. "This is my — uh — assistant." He introduced Rina.

"Oh." The worker seemed nervous. "Were you sent by Omaha?"

"No," Dolf said. "We're stationed on an emergency spaceship. We were curious about asteroid mining. Neither of us is familiar with it. So our captain left us here while he makes a delivery to headquarters."

"Yes," one of the other workers said, "I heard they were delivering the ingots by ship now."

"How long has your crew been here?" Dolf asked. "We understand you all came together."

Several of the crew members exchanged glances.

"That's right," one of them said. "We've been a crew for a long time. We always work together. We like it that way."

Dolf nodded and didn't say any more.

That night, Orel informed them that another space tug was loaded and ready.

"We're going to take a chance and launch it in the morning," she said. "But I'm not telling any of

the crew until the time of the launch. They have been told everything is leaving by spaceship."

"Are there other ships coming?" Dolf asked. "It will be a week before Druce and the EM 88 return."

"Yes," Orel said. "They are sending two ships a day. But I want to see what happens."

It was still dark the next morning when Dolf and Rina joined Orel at the launch station.

"The space tug is ready, Orel," one of the workers announced. "Shall we take it over to the ship dock?"

"No," Orel said. "We're going to launch."

"But I thought . . ." the worker began.

"I've changed my mind," Orel said. "Launch it."

Within a matter of minutes, the space tug had taken off for its trip through orbit to headquarters.

"How do you monitor them?" Dolf asked.

"There's an electronic device aboard," Orel said. "Unfortunately, it only tells us when the shipment slips out of orbit. It doesn't tell us where it's going."

"Have you thought of photographing it?" Dolf said.

"We've tried," Orel said. "But unless we follow it all the way, it's no good. There's no point in putting a camera on board. It would just get lost with the shipment."

"Maybe we can follow one with the EM 88 when they return," Rina suggested.

"In the meantime," Orel said, "we have to get back to work. We will need a full tug for the spaceship arriving this afternoon."

Dolf and Rina spent the day helping out where they could, trying to keep an eye on everyone and everything. Neither of them saw anything unusual.

They were sitting in Orel's office, waiting for the spaceship, when Zelig came rushing in.

"Orel, I need you."

Dolf and Rina jumped up.

Zelig swung around. "No." His voice was harsh. "You stay here."

He hurried Orel out of the room.

Dolf and Rina stared at each other. "Now what?" Dolf wondered.

In a few moments, Orel returned. Her face was grave.

"Someone is stealing the ingots," she said.

"Stealing them! Right here on the asteroid?" Dolf asked.

"The shipment is light. There's no doubt about it. I've checked it myself."

Orel dropped into her chair. "Well, now we know that the problem is right here."

"Why wouldn't Zelig let us go with you?" Rina asked.

Orel gave a little laugh. "He didn't know where you had come from. You're the only strangers around. He thought you were responsible. I told him it wasn't possible."

"I have an idea," Rina said. "What time is the evening meal?"

"1800," Orel said. "Why?"

"And where does that strange crew eat? In their own quarters?"

"Yes," Orel said. "Their supplies come on a special spaceship."

Dolf stared at her. "Doesn't that seem strange to you?"

"I told you," Orel explained. "They're from Omaha. They have special orders."

"I can understand special orders," Dolf said. "But why special food?"

"I don't know," Orel admitted. "I assumed they were getting some kind of information along with their supplies."

"I'm going to check into this tonight," Rina said.

As soon as they had finished the evening meal, she put on her spacesuit once again.

"I'll be back," she said to Dolf.

"Wait," he said. "I'll go with you."

"No." She shook her head. "It will be much easier for one of us to go unseen. If we're both there . . ." She didn't finish her sentence.

She left the living quarters and went out into the dark, starlit night. She had a strange sense of floating in space. Stars surrounded her as she made her way to the strange spaceship.

When she reached the huge vessel, she moved quietly around it. With her supersight, she was able to examine it closely.

A small window was cut into the rear of the

ship. Rina crept up close. She gripped one of the landing legs and inched her way up. When she reached the window, she peered inside.

The strange crew were sitting around a black stone table. Rina gasped as she saw their faces. Their skin had a green pasty hue to it. Their heads were completely bald. They had small ear openings, but no visible ear-shaped tissue. The crew were not Earth men!

Rina slid back down the leg and ran back toward Orel's office. But the building was closed.

"Where can she be?" Rina wondered. "I must see her at once."

She went to the living quarters where she and Dolf had been assigned rooms. She asked the first worker she saw if he knew where Orel's room was. He directed her to the first building in the row.

"She has her own room there," he said.

Rina stopped to get Dolf. She told him briefly what she had seen.

When they arrived at Orel's place, Rina described everything in detail.

"They are humanoids," she said. "But they are definitely not from Earth."

"Why did Omaha send them up here?" Orel wondered.

"Are you sure Omaha sent them?" Dolf asked.

"I have their orders over at headquarters. The papers were all legal."

"I'd like to see them if I can," Dolf said.

When they got to Orel's office, the papers were gone.

"I don't understand this."

"I do," Dolf said grimly. "The papers were forged. That supply ship that comes in — have you ever seen the people who unload it?"

Orel shook her head. "I've never paid any attention. I don't think anyone else has, either."

"Of course not," Dolf agreed. "With spacesuits on, everyone looks alike. They knew that no one would ever question them."

"But what are they doing with the ingots?" Rina asked. "We should find out."

"We'd better wait until Druce returns," Dolf said. "In the meantime, we'll keep an eye on them."

For the rest of the week, Dolf and Rina took turns observing the strange crew.

"Do you think they know we're watching?" Rina asked one morning.

Dolf shook his head. "I doubt it. We've been busy helping the miners. I don't think they can tell us from anyone else in our suits."

The following day, the EM 88 returned.

"Well," Druce said when Dolf and Rina were back on board, "have you found out anything?"

"We have," Dolf said, and told him about the strange creatures.

"Why didn't you notify headquarters at once?" Druce asked.

"Because we were afraid they could monitor our space-tel," Dolf said. "We don't know what kind of equipment they have. We don't even know who they are or where they're from!" he exclaimed.

Druce thought for a moment. "You're probably right. Have any more shipments been lost?"

"No," Rina said. "Orel has launched several, but they've all arrived safely."

"But ingots are missing," Dolf said.

"What do you mean, missing?"

"They must be stealing off the top," Dolf explained. "Rina and I think they must have almost a tugfull by now."

"Have they any weapons?" Druce asked.

"We don't know," Dolf said.

"If they have a tugfull of ingots," Druce said, "they must be planning on doing something with them. What time do they launch from up here?"

"They launch several times a day," Rina explained. "But only the 0600 launches ever get lost. We figured that out when we first got here."

"Then that's the time we'll watch the launch pad," Druce said. "We'll stay docked here until we find out what's going on. I'm going to send headquarters a coded message."

For the next two mornings, Dolf and Rina and Druce watched the launch pad. Nothing happened. Other spaceships came in every day to pick up the tugs filled with ingots.

One of the EM ship captains brought Druce a message from Commander Markey at headquarters. Druce read it quickly.

"He wants us to bring the strange crew to headquarters." He gave a short laugh. "He has no suggestions about how to do it."

"I know how to do it," Rina said. "When you're ready, let me know."

Druce looked at her, but she laughed and shook her head.

"I'll tell you when the time comes," she said.

"How much longer are we going to keep up the morning watch, Druce?" Dolf wanted to know.

"Until we catch them at something," Druce muttered. "They have to make a move soon. Their whole ship will be loaded with ingots before long."

The next morning Druce and Dolf were out at 0500 watching the launch pad. An hour later, they were about to leave when Rina came running up.

"Quick!" she whispered. "They're going to launch their tug of ingots."

Druce jumped up. "What are you talking about?"

"I decided to watch their ship while you were

watching here," she said. "They have their own launch mechanism. It's nothing like ours. Hurry." She led them back toward the strange spaceship.

They hid behind one of the temporary work buildings.

"There," Rina whispered. "Look!"

The strange crew was at the rear of their dock area.

"Good planning," Druce whispered. "No one can see them from the other parts of the asteroid."

"Exactly," Rina said. "That's why they picked this place to dock."

Just as the crew was about to launch the tug, Druce met them.

"Stop!" he ordered. "I am here on the authority of Universe headquarters. I command you to stop."

The startled figures spun around. Druce motioned them toward the EM 88.

"Get aboard," he ordered.

One of the figures started to run in the opposite direction.

"Return," one of the other strange creatures ordered. "Where can you go?"

"That's right," Druce said. "You can't escape from here."

As he was leading the group toward his ship, he saw Rina slip behind the strange spaceship.

"Dolf, help me take these people aboard," he said. "Then go see what Rina is doing."

When the creatures were aboard the EM 88, Druce questioned them briefly.

"Can you survive in our environment?" he asked.

One of the creatures nodded his head yes.

"Then please remove your spacesuits," Druce ordered.

"We prefer not to do that, captain," the man who seemed to be their leader said.

"Do as I say or I will have it done for you." Druce kept his voice even.

Slowly, the creatures shed their suits. Druce saw that Rina's description of them was accurate.

"Who are you?" he demanded. "Where are you from?"

"We are from Gonda," the leader said.

"Gonda!" Druce exclaimed. "But that's in another galaxy! We only know about Gonda through radio communication."

"Yes," the leader agreed.

"And you have the capability to enter our galaxy?" Druce was astounded.

The leader smiled. "We have many capabilities you know nothing of," he answered. "We can do many things you are not able to do."

"You are coming back to headquarters with us," Druce answered.

"No, captain. You are wrong." The leader motioned to the men to put their spacesuits on again. "We are leaving now. We are returning to our ship. There is nothing you can do to stop us."

Druce knew he was right.

"Just a moment," he said. "Before you leave, one question. Why were you stealing the ingots?"

"Gonda sits at the break between our galaxies," the leader explained. "Our galaxy is much older than yours. Our supplies of ore are running out. We knew you were mining here. We have been monitoring you for a great amount of time. We decided to use some of your ore."

"But how did you manage it?" Druce asked. "I still don't understand."

The leader made the same smiling face. "It was simple. The tug was launched with your monitor on it. But there was also a future orbit finder on it. We installed that. It sent the ingots to Gonda. When our supply ship came in, the finder was returned to us. We then put it in our next shipment. And now, captain —" the man made a small bow — "I'm afraid we must leave you. Our mining days are over."

He motioned to his crew, and they followed him out of the EM 88.

Druce ran after them.

Dolf and Rina were standing outside the ship. Orel came out of her office.

"What happened?" Dolf cried.

Druce told them who the creatures were.

"There's nothing I can do to stop them leaving," Druce said.

"But they've stolen the ore!" Orel protested.

"We can't prove it," Druce said. "And we don't have authority over them. They're not of our galaxy."

The creatures disappeared inside their spaceship.

Druce sighed. "I don't know what headquarters will say about this," he said.

Rina laughed. "They'll probably give you a hero's medal."

Druce looked at her. "For letting them get away?"

"But they're not getting away," Rina said. "Watch."

The strange spaceship continued to sit quietly in its dock.

"I don't understand," Druce said. "I thought they would take off immediately."

"They can't," Rina said. "I told you I'd fix it so you could take them back to headquarters."

Dolf turned to her. "Rina, what did you do?"

She showed them a large metal container. She

had hidden it alongside the EM 88.

"What is that?" Druce asked.

"It's their power system," Rina said. "While you had them here, I went around and removed it."

"But how did you know . . ." Dolf began.

Rina raised an eyebrow. "You forget, Dolf, I can see a lot more than most people. I spotted the power system the first time I examined the ship."

"Orel," Druce said quickly, "we're leaving. I don't think you'll have any more trouble. Rina, Dolf, board the ship."

He hustled them inside.

"But, Druce!" Dolf protested.

"Don't argue with me," Druce said. "I know what I'm doing."

As soon as they were back aboard, Druce ordered the ship sealed. He ran up to Brita's pilot cabin.

"How soon can you take off?" he asked.

"Whenever you want."

"I want now!" he demanded.

She looked startled. "This minute?"

"This minute," he declared. "Get off!"

Within seconds, Brita was ready to lift the huge space vehicle off of the launching pad. Druce got on the space ship intercom.

"Ivo," he yelled, "are you there?"

The engineer's voice came up from the third level. "Right here, Druce. What is it?"

"Activate the magnetic space harness," Druce ordered.

"Right away. What are we carrying?" Ivo asked.

"Another spaceship," Druce said, and flipped off the intercom.

Brita steered the EM 88 over the strange space ship. Ivo attached the magnetic space harness. Before the Gonda creatures knew what was happening, they were lifted into the atmosphere.

As they took off into space, Dolf looked at Rina and laughed.

"Well," he said, "maybe they have some capabilities that we don't have, but this time I think we're one up on them."

The EM 88 moved swiftly through space toward the headquarters Astro-lab ahead.

# Enter the final frontier.

## Read:

PLANET OF ICE
FORGOTTEN WORLD
SILENT INVADERS
GREEN INVASION
MEDICAL EMERGENCY
STRANGERS ON NMA-6
METEOR FROM THE MOON
UNWANTED VISITORS
MYSTERY ON MARS

GALAXY I
JOURNEY INTO THE FUTURE